WORRY SAYS
WHAT?

To all children who
have ever felt worried.
You are not alone.

– Allison

DUPLICATION AND COPYRIGHT

NATIONAL CENTER for
YOUTH ISSUES

P.O. Box 22185
Chattanooga, TN 37422-2185
423-899-5714 • 866-318-6294
fax 423-899-4547 • www.ncyi.org

ISBN: 978-1-937870-51-5 $9.95
Library of Congress Control Number: 2018954437
© 2018 National Center for Youth Issues, Chattanooga, TN
All rights reserved.
Written by: Allison Edwards
Illustrations by: Ayesha L. Rubio
Published by National Center for Youth Issues • Softcover
Printed at Starkey Printing, Chattanooga, Tennessee, U.S.A., October 2019

There is a place inside my brain where Worry likes to set up camp.
In the back, far out of sight, I hear him putting up a tent and chopping
wood for a fire. He hums a little tune while he's working.

Worry's songs tie my tummy up in knots,
and the things he says make my heart beat very fast.

Sometimes he speaks in a whisper,
and other times his voice gets so loud
I can't hear anything else.

Like when I take a math test.
At first, Worry whispers,
"It's too hard."

Then his voice gets louder...
so loud I can't even think.

I try to concentrate,
but Worry keeps saying
over and over,

"It's too hard!
You can't do it!
You'll never get it right!"

Maybe Worry is right. I don't know how to do this math.
I lay down my pencil and watch as everyone else finishes their test.

When I want to play with the other kids at recess,
Worry starts talking as I walk toward them.
I try to hum to myself so I can't hear what he's saying,
but Worry's voice drowns out mine.
First Worry says, "They don't like you."

Then Worry begins singing his own song.

♪

"They think you're weird…dee dee dee.

♩

You'll never fit in…la la la.

♫

They don't want to play with you…da da da." ♪

When I try to do a back handspring in gymnastics,
Worry starts up again; his voice booming and constant as I walk onto the mat.

Worry insists, "You're not strong enough."

"You'll fall. Everyone will laugh at you.

You're gonna get hurt!"

Maybe Worry is right. Maybe I should stop trying. I go to the edge of the mat and watch my friends do roundoffs and cartwheels without me.

When I crawl into bed at night and shut my eyes,
I hear Worry's voice again. He whispers, "You're not safe."

I listen closely to the noises in the house as Worry asks,

"Do you wonder what's making that sound?

Is there something in the closet?

What's that shadow on the ceiling?"

I'm too scared to sleep.

Tired from all the worrying, I confront him. "Will I always be afraid?"
"You will if you keep listening to me," Worry says.

The truth is, listening to Worry is ruining my life.
He never makes me feel better. He always makes me worse.

And right then, I decide one thing.

I am DONE letting Worry be the boss of me!

The next day, I get up, and instead of waiting
for Worry to talk to me, I start talking to Worry.

As I walk to school, I tell Worry it's time for him to go. Every time he tries to talk to me, I ignore him.

In a voice, clear and loud, I tell myself what is true.

When I walk into math class, I say,
"I can do hard things!"

And I raise my hand to solve the hardest math problem
Mrs. Johnson puts on the board.

When I go outside at recess, I say,
"I have lots of friends!"

And I ask Lily if she wants
to swing with me.

When I walk into gymnastics,
I say, "**I believe in myself!**"

My first back handspring doesn't go so well,
and I hear Worry, suddenly right behind me.

"See, I told you!

You can't do it!"

I look right into his eyes and yell, "I can't yet, but I will!"
And I keep doing them over and over until I master the back handspring.

Then I head to the balance beam…
because I can do anything I put my mind to!

That night, when I'm getting ready for bed,
I declare, "**I am not afraid.**"

Worry says,
"What? I didn't hear you."

I say it again, even louder this time. **"I AM NOT AFRAID!"**

7:08

"Then I'll find someone else who will listen to me."
As Worry packs up his tent to leave, I realize how
much smaller he's gotten.

I know he'll be back again, and I'll be ready.

Every now and then, I hear Worry chopping wood for his fire and putting tent poles together.
Before he can even get settled back in, I sing a little song, just loud enough for him to hear.

"I can do hard things . . . da da da da da.

I have lots of friends . . . la la la la la.

I believe in myself . . . do do do do do.

I am not afraid . . . ha ha ha ha ha."

Worry says **what?**

Worry says **nothing**.

Tips for Helping Children Overcome Worry

Children have a number of worries throughout their childhood that will come and go. The problem is not with the worries themselves, but that children believe the worries to be true. Children will only be able to overcome their worries if they stop listening to the voice in their head that tells them they can't do it, they won't succeed, or that things will never get better.

Here are three ways to empower children to overcome worry:

1. **Ask children to develop a counter statement to their worry.** If worry tells them they **can't** do something, have them say, "I **can** do _____." They can write the statement on their school notebook or make a poster and hang it in their bedroom. Have them repeat it over and over until they believe it to be true.

2. **Help children make an "I Did It!" list when they overcome a fear.** Have them write down their name, the date, and the fear they were able to overcome so they will have a record of their successes. Hang it in a visible place so they are constantly reminded of how strong they are.

3. **Have children give their worry a name.** A name such as "Worry Walter" will help take the power out of the fear. Instead of saying, "I'm too afraid to take the test," a child can say, "Worry Walter came to visit and he's telling me that I won't do well on the test." Then they can tell Worry Walter to go away and not come back.